To Andrew McIsaac of
Cookstown, Ontario and
to Andrew Munsch of
Guelph, Ontario

One day Andrew's mother and father were taking him to see his grandma and grandpa. Before they put him in the car his mother said, "Andrew, do you have to go pee?"

Andrew said, "**NO, NO, NO, NO, NO.**"

His father said, very slowly and clearly, "Andrew, do you have to go pee?"

"**NO, NO, NO, NO,**" said Andrew. "I have decided never to go pee again."

So they put Andrew into the car, fastened his seatbelt and gave him lots of books, and lots of toys, and lots of crayons, and drove off down the road—
VAROOMMM.

They had been driving for just one minute when Andrew yelled, "**I HAVE TO GO PEE!**"

"**YIKES,**" said the father.

"**OH NO,**" said the mother.

Then the father said, "Now, Andrew, wait just five minutes. In five minutes we will come to a gas station where you can go pee."

Andrew said, "I have to go pee **RIGHT NOW!**"

So the mother stopped the car—**SCREEEEECH.**

Andrew jumped out of the car and peed behind a bush.

When they got to Grandma's and Grandpa's house, Andrew wanted to go out to play. It was snowing, and he needed a snowsuit. Before they put on the snowsuit, the mother and the father and the grandma and the grandpa all said,

"ANDREW! DO YOU HAVE TO GO PEE?"

Andrew said, "NO, NO, NO, NO, NO."

So they put on Andrew's snowsuit. It had five zippers, 10 buckles and 17 snaps. It took them half an hour to get the snowsuit on.

Andrew walked out into the back yard, threw one snowball and yelled, "I HAVE TO GO PEE."

The father and the mother and the grandma and the grandpa all ran outside, got Andrew out of the snowsuit, and carried him to the bathroom.

So his mother gave him a kiss, and his father gave him a kiss, and his grandma gave him a kiss, and his grandpa gave him a kiss.

"Just wait," said the mother, "he's going to yell and say he has to go pee."

"Oh," said the father, "he does it every night. It's driving me crazy."

The grandmother said, "I never had these problems with my children."

They waited for five minutes, 10 minutes, 15 minutes, 20 minutes.

When Andrew came back down they had a nice long dinner. Then it was time for Andrew to go to bed.

Before they put Andrew into bed, the mother and the father and the grandma and the grandpa all said,
"ANDREW! DO YOU HAVE TO GO PEE?"

Andrew said, "NO, NO, NO, NO, NO."

The father said, "I think he is asleep."

The mother said, "Yes, I think he is asleep."

The grandmother said, "He is definitely asleep and he didn't yell and say he had to go pee."

Then Andrew said, "I wet my bed."

So the mother and the father and the grandma and the grandpa all changed Andrew's bed and Andrew's pajamas. Then the mother gave him a kiss, and the father gave him a kiss, and the grandma gave him a kiss, and the grandpa gave him a kiss, and the grownups all went downstairs.

They waited five minutes, 10 minutes, 15 minutes, 20 minutes, and from upstairs Andrew yelled,

"GRANDPA, DO YOU HAVE TO GO PEE?"

And Grandpa said, "Why, yes, I think I do."

Andrew said, "Well, so do I."

So they both went to the bathroom and peed in the toilet, and Andrew did not wet his bed again that night, not even once.

Even More Classic Munsch:

The Dark
Mud Puddle
The Paper Bag Princess
The Boy in the Drawer
Jonathan Cleaned Up—Then He Heard a Sound
Murmel, Murmel, Murmel
Millicent and the Wind
Mortimer
Pigs
The Fire Station
Angela's Airplane
David's Father
Thomas' Snowsuit
50 Below Zero
Moira's Birthday
A Promise is a Promise
Something Good
Show and Tell
Purple, Green and Yellow
Wait and See
Where is Gah-Ning?
From Far Away
Stephanie's Ponytail
Munschworks: The First Munsch Collection
Munschworks 2: The Second Munsch Treasury
Munschworks 3: The Third Munsch Treasury
Munschworks 4: The Fourth Munsch Treasury
The Munschworks Grand Treasury
Munsch Mini-Treasury One
Munsch Mini-Treasury Two
Munsch Mini-Treasury Three
Classic Munsch ABC
Classic Munsch 123

For information on these titles please visit www.annickpress.com
Many Munsch titles are available in French and/or Spanish, as well as in
board book and e-book editions. Please contact your favorite supplier.

More MUNSCH to enjoy!

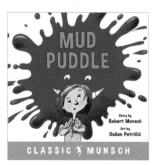

SHOW AND TELL

Story by Robert Munsch

Art by Michael Martchenko

CLASSIC MUNSCH

PIGS

Story by Robert Munsch   Art by Michael Martchenko

CLASSIC MUNSCH

DAVID'S FATHER

Story by Robert Munsch   Art by Michael Martchenko

CLASSIC MUNSCH

WAIT AND SEE

Story by Robert Munsch

Art by Michael Martchenko

CLASSIC MUNSCH

The **Paper Bag Princess**

Story by Robert Munsch   Art by Michael Martchenko

CLASSIC MUNSCH

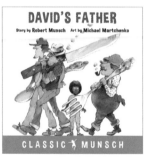

MUD PUDDLE

Story by Robert Munsch

Art by Dušan Petričić

CLASSIC MUNSCH

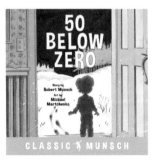

50 BELOW ZERO

Story by Robert Munsch

Art by Michael Martchenko

CLASSIC MUNSCH